Usborne Farmyard Tales

The
Snow Storm

Heather Amery

Illustrated by Stephen Cartwright

Language consultant: Betty Root
Series editor: Jenny Tyler

There is a little yellow duck to find on every page.

This is Apple Tree Farm.

This is Mrs. Boot, the farmer. She has two children,
called Poppy and Sam, and a dog called Rusty.

In the night there was a big snow storm.

In the morning, it is still snowing. "You must wrap up warm," says Mrs. Boot to Poppy and Sam.

Ted works on the farm.

He helps Mrs. Boot look after the animals.
He gives them food and water every day.

"Come and help me," calls Ted.

"Where are you going?" says Poppy. "I'm taking this hay to the sheep," says Ted.

Poppy and Sam pull the hay.

They go out of the farmyard with Ted. They walk to the gate of the sheep field.

"Where are the sheep?" says Sam.

"They are all covered with snow," says Ted.
"We'll have to find them," says Poppy.

They brush the snow off the sheep.

Ted, Poppy and Sam give each sheep lots of hay.
"They've got nice warm coats," says Sam.

Poppy counts the sheep.

"There are only six sheep. One is missing," says
Poppy. "It's that naughty Woolly," says Ted.

They look for Woolly.

They walk around the snowy field. "Rusty, good
dog, find Woolly," calls Sam.

Rusty runs across the field.

Ted, Poppy and Sam run after him. Rusty barks
at the thick hedge.

Ted looks under the hedge.

"Can you see anything?" says Sam. "Yes, Woolly is hiding in there. Clever Rusty," says Ted.

"Come on, Woolly."

"Let me help you out, old girl," says Ted.
Carefully he pulls Woolly out of the hedge.

"There's something else!"

"Look, I can see something moving," says Sam.
"What is it, Ted?" says Poppy.

Ted lifts out a tiny lamb.

"Woolly has had a lamb," he says. "We'll take it and Woolly to the barn. They'll be warm there."

Poppy rides home.

She holds the lamb. "What a surprise!" she says.
"Good old Woolly."

Cover design by Hannah Ahmed   Digital manipulation by Nelupa Hussain

This edition first published in 2004 by Usborne Publishing Ltd, 83-85 Saffron Hill, London EC1N 8RT, England. www.usborne.com